D1218112

script:
ANDREW DABB

pencils:
CHRIS LIE

inks:
RAMANDA KAMARGA

colors:
ROB RUFFOLO

lettering:
BRIAN J. CROWLEY

editor:
MIKE O'SULLIVAN

CODENAME: SNAKE-EYES
SPECIALITY:
ENEMY INFILTRATION

CODENAME: STORM SHADOW
SPECIALITY: SABOTAGE
OPERATIONS

KUMITE

Spotlight

DDP

visit us at www.abdopublishing.com

Exclusive reinforced library bound edition published in 2008 by Spotlight, a division of ABDO Publishing Group, Edina, Minnesota. This edition is produced under agreement with Devils Due Publishing, Inc. www.devilsdue.net

Library of Congress Cataloging-in-Publication Data

Dabb, Andrew.
   Kumite / script, Andrew Dabb ; pencils, Chris Lie ; inks, Ramanda Kamarga ; colors, Rob Ruffolo ; lettering, Brian J. Crowley ; editor, Mike O'Sullivan. -- Exclusive reinforced library bound ed.
     p. cm. -- (G.I. Joe SIGMA 6)
   Revision of issue 6 (May 2006) of G.I. Joe Sigma 6.
   ISBN-13: 978-1-59961-373-4
   ISBN-10: 1-59961-373-5
   1. Graphic novels. I. Lie, Chris. II. O'Sullivan, Mike. III. G.I. Joe SIGMA 6. 6. IV. Title.

PN6727.D23 K86 2008
741.5'973--dc22

2006038492

All Spotlight books have reinforced library bindings
and are manufactured in the United States of America.

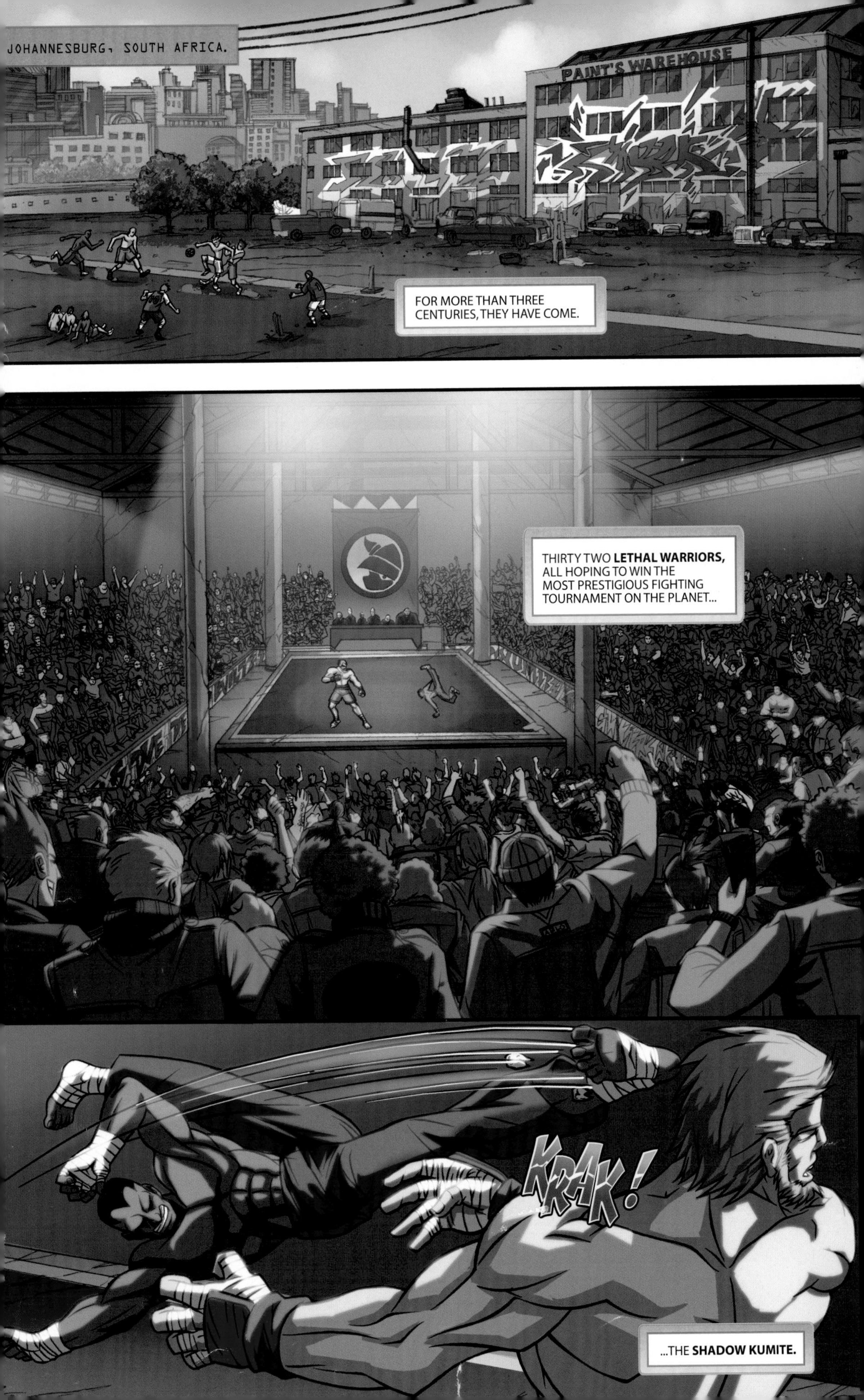
JOHANNESBURG, SOUTH AFRICA.
PAINT'S WAREHOUSE
FOR MORE THAN THREE CENTURIES, THEY HAVE COME.
THIRTY TWO **LETHAL WARRIORS,** ALL HOPING TO WIN THE MOST PRESTIGIOUS FIGHTING TOURNAMENT ON THE PLANET...
KRAK!
...THE **SHADOW KUMITE.**

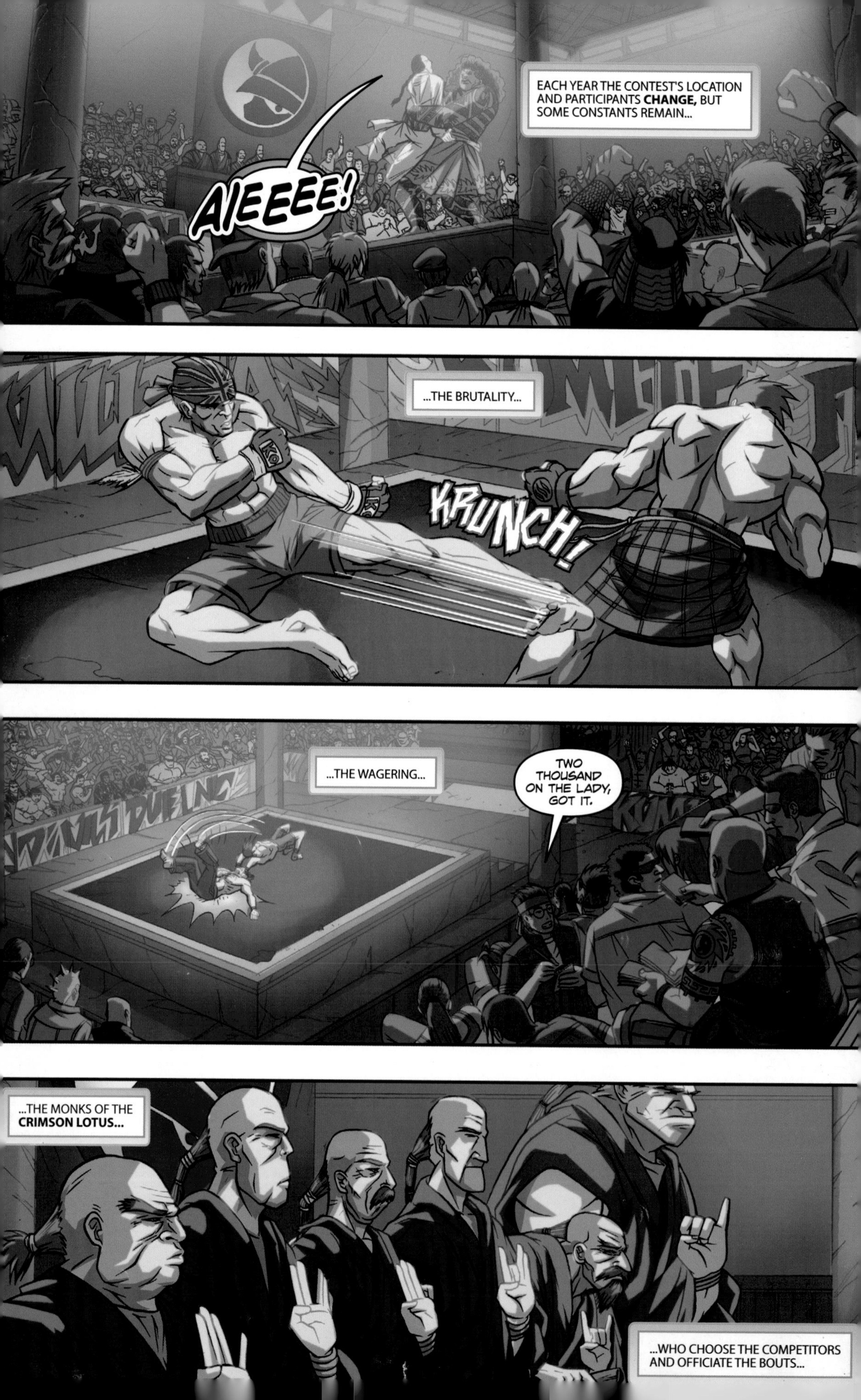
EACH YEAR THE CONTEST'S LOCATION AND PARTICIPANTS **CHANGE,** BUT SOME CONSTANTS REMAIN...
AIEEEEE!
...THE BRUTALITY...
KRUNCH!
...THE WAGERING...
TWO THOUSAND ON THE LADY, GOT IT.
...THE MONKS OF THE **CRIMSON LOTUS...**
...WHO CHOOSE THE COMPETITORS AND OFFICIATE THE BOUTS...

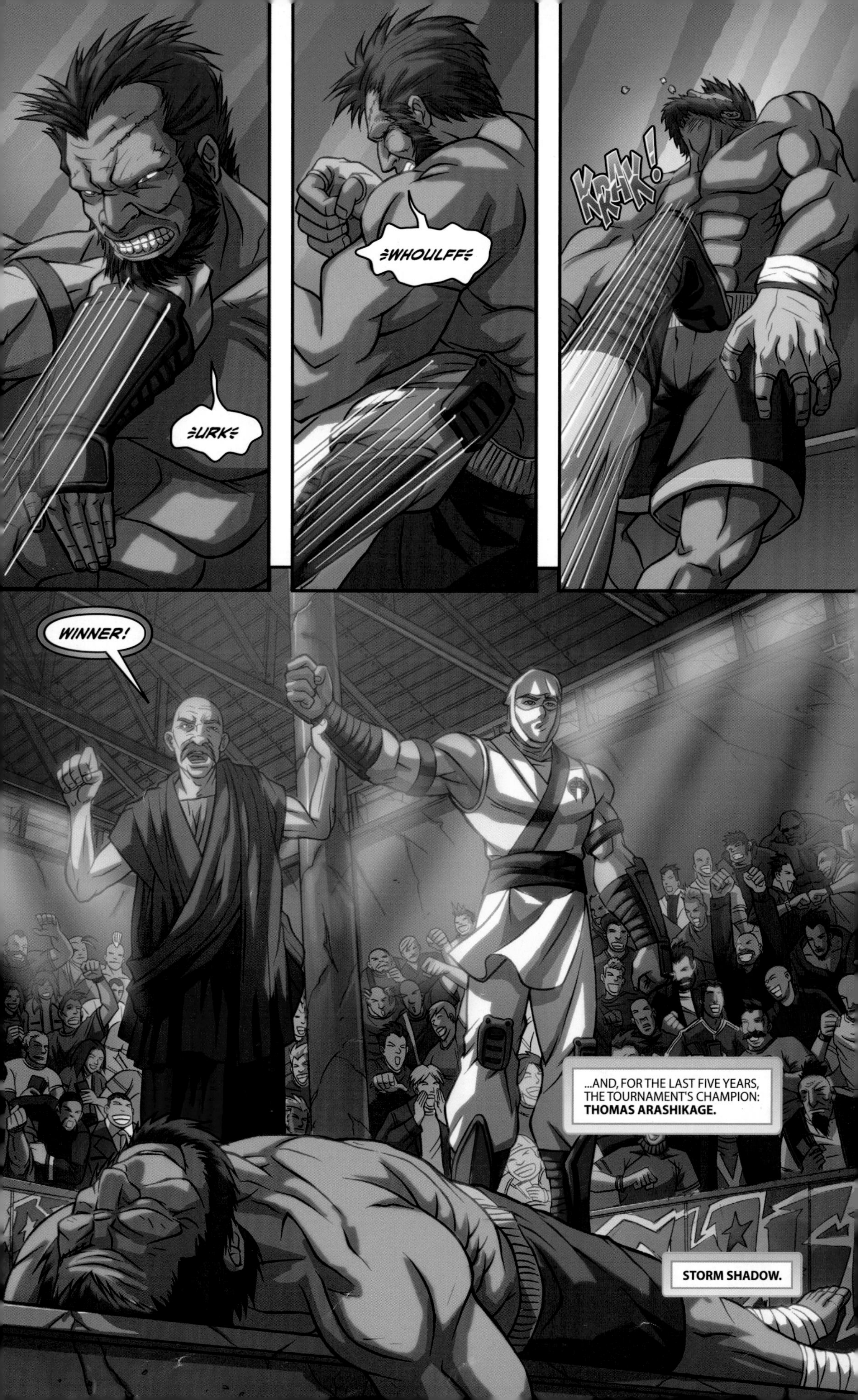
URK
WHOULFF
KRAK!
WINNER!
...AND, FOR THE LAST FIVE YEARS, THE TOURNAMENT'S CHAMPION: THOMAS ARASHIKAGE.
STORM SHADOW.

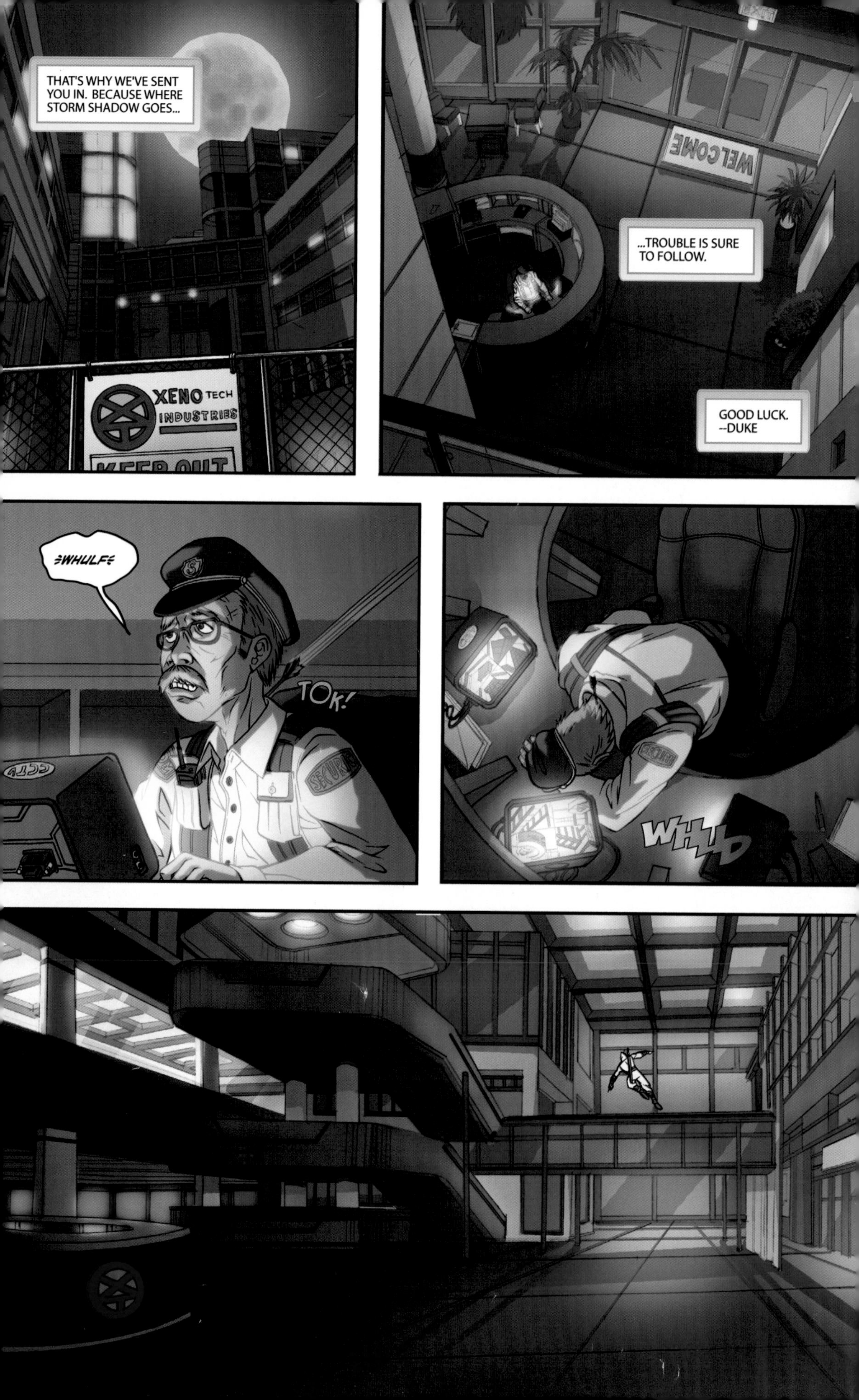
THAT'S WHY WE'VE SENT YOU IN. BECAUSE WHERE STORM SHADOW GOES...
XENO TECH INDUSTRIES
KEEP OUT
WELCOME
...TROUBLE IS SURE TO FOLLOW.
GOOD LUCK. --DUKE
WHULF
TOK!
WHUD

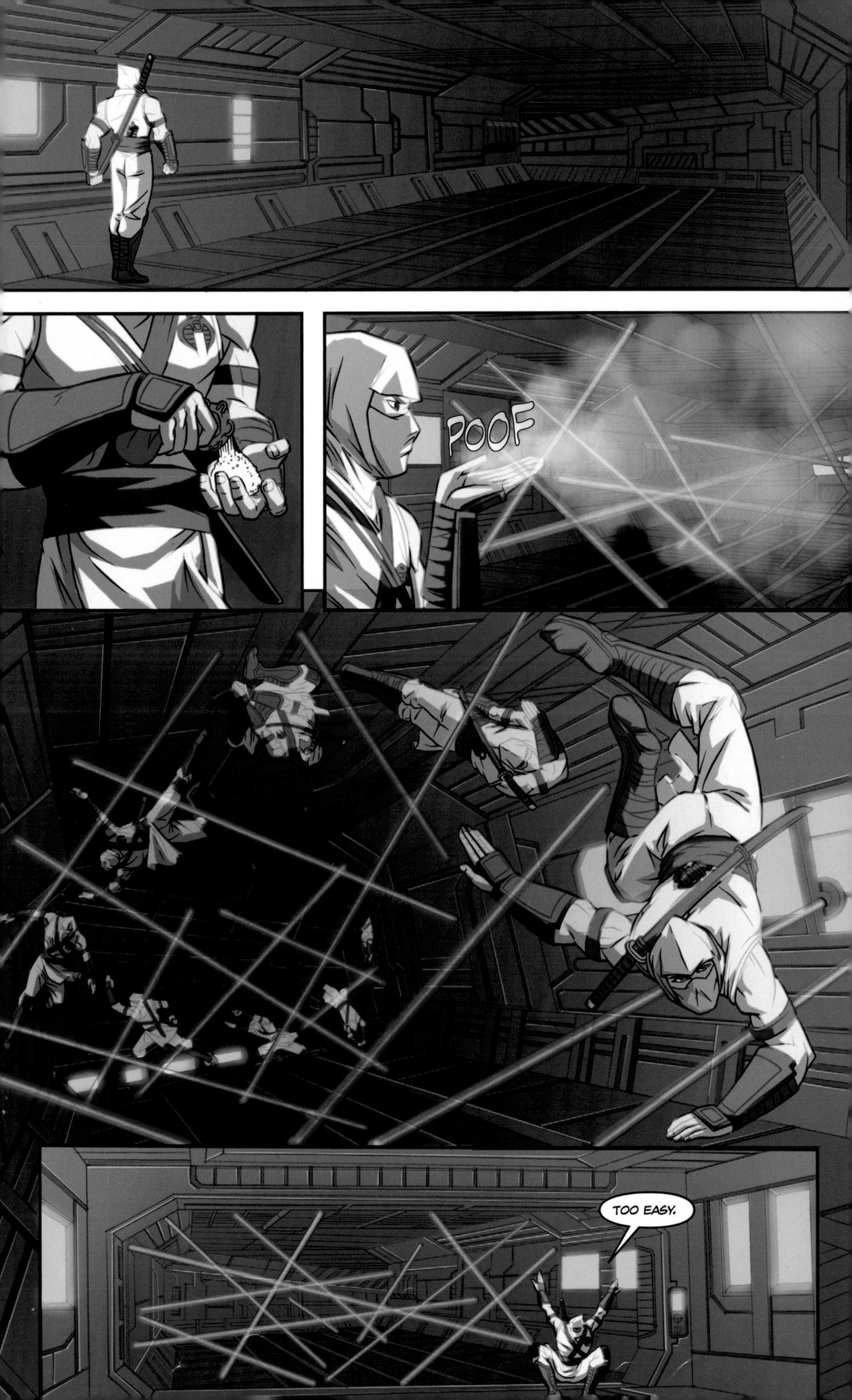
POOF
TOO EASY.

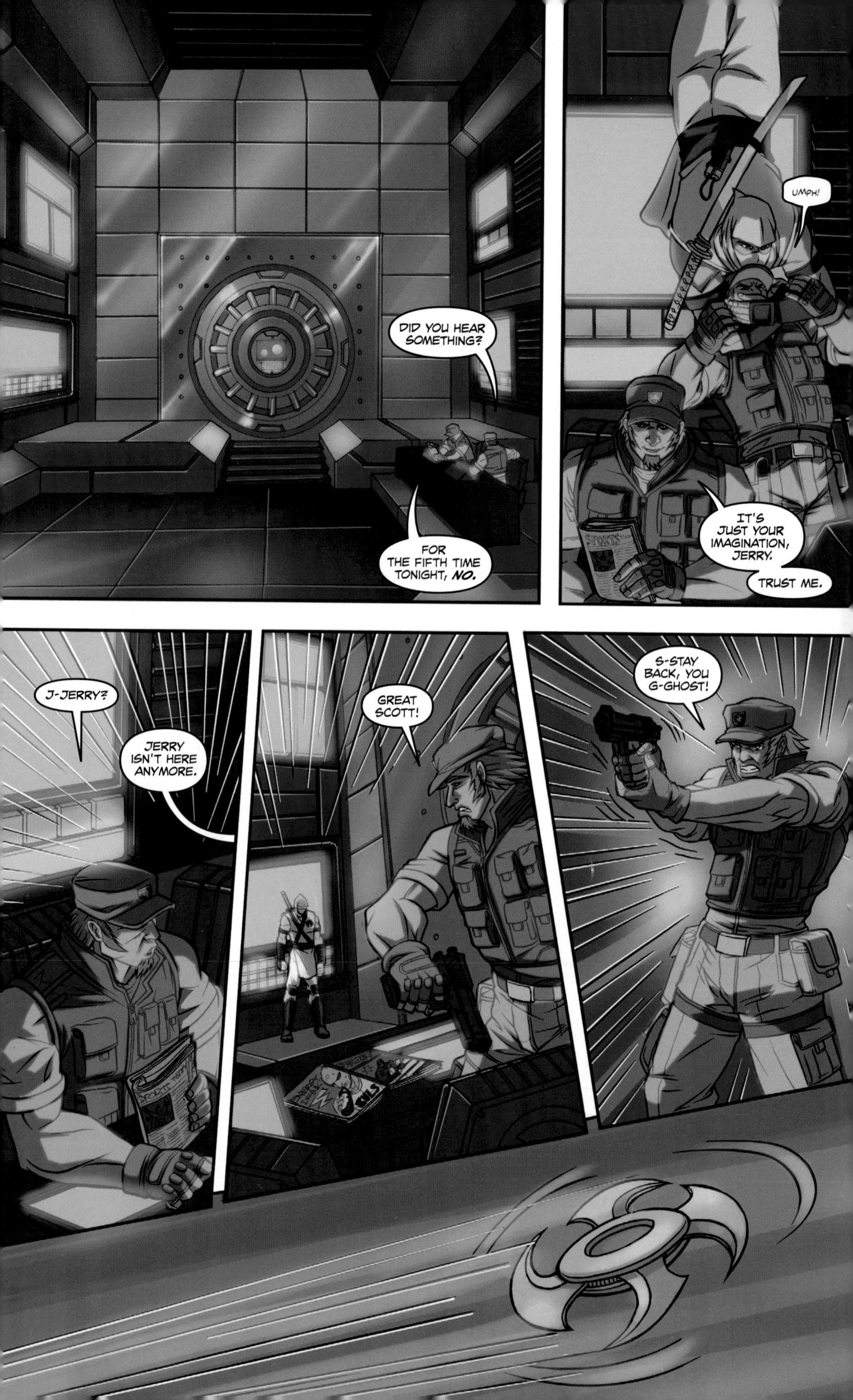
DID YOU HEAR SOMETHING?
FOR THE FIFTH TIME TONIGHT, NO.
UMPH!
IT'S JUST YOUR IMAGINATION, JERRY.
TRUST ME.
J-JERRY?
JERRY ISN'T HERE ANYMORE.
GREAT SCOTT!
S-STAY BACK, YOU G-GHOST!

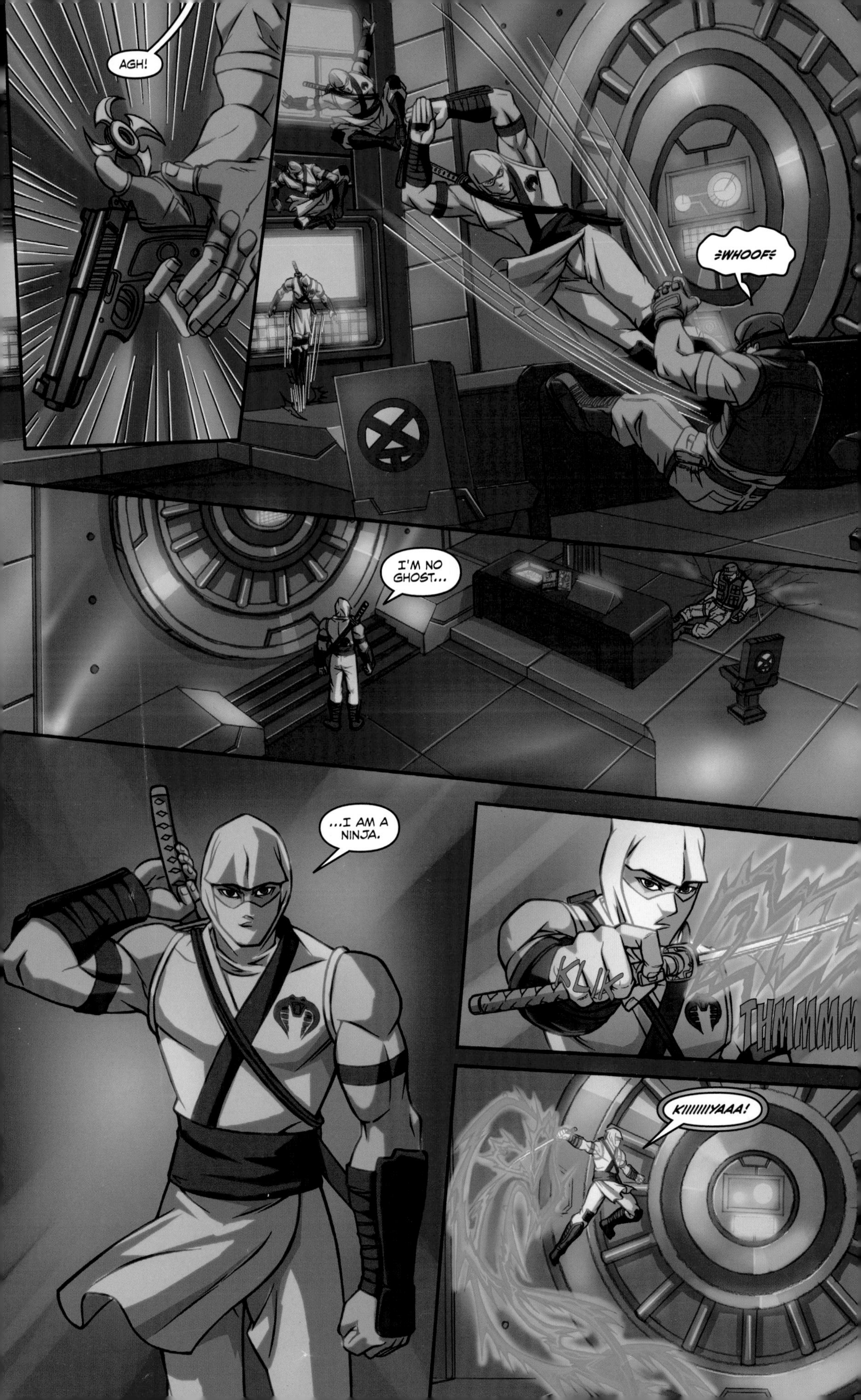
AGH!
WHOOF
I'M NO GHOST...
...I AM A NINJA.
KLIK
THMMMM
KIIIIIIYAAA!

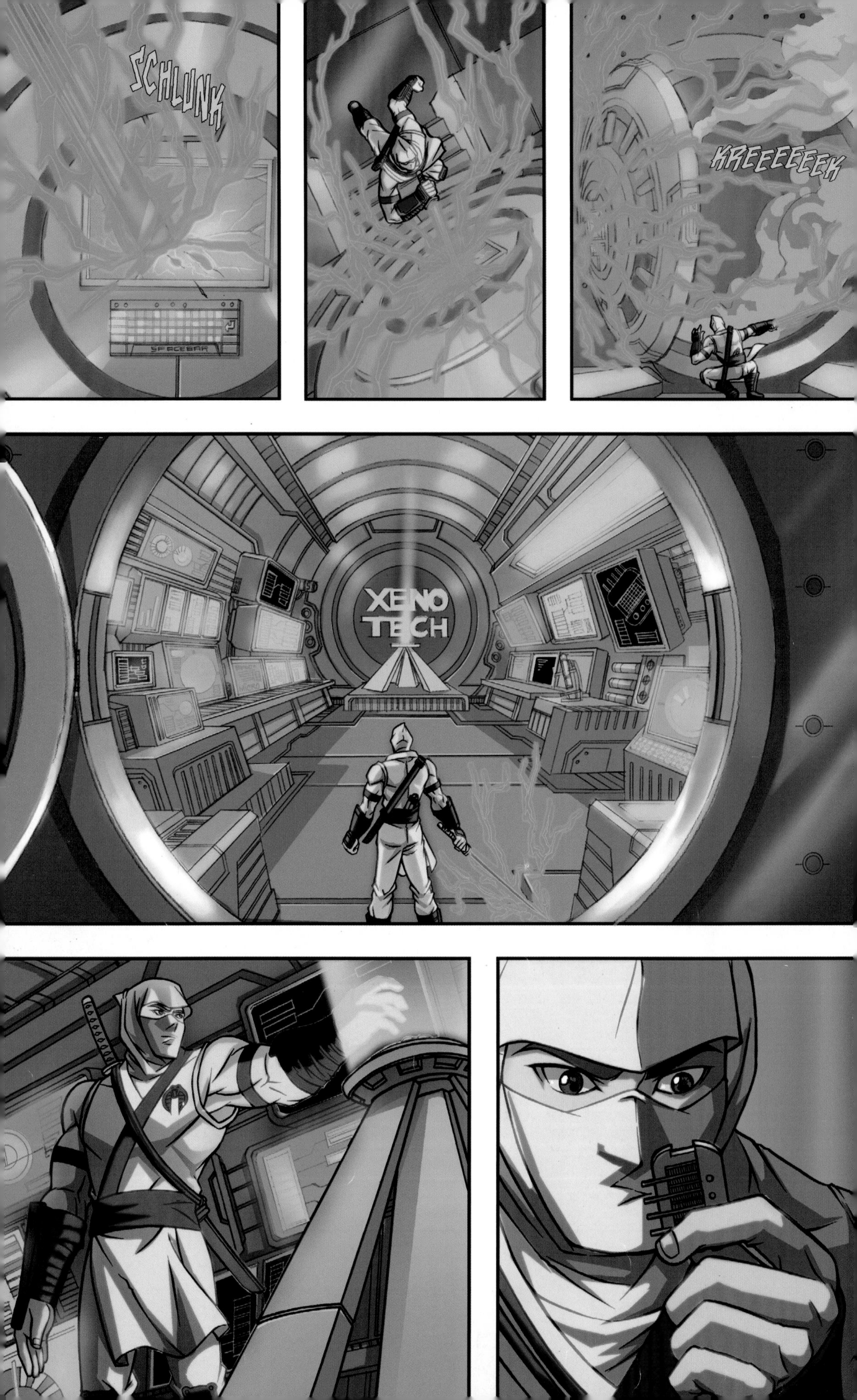
SCHLUNK
SPACEBAR
KREEEEEEK
XENO TECH

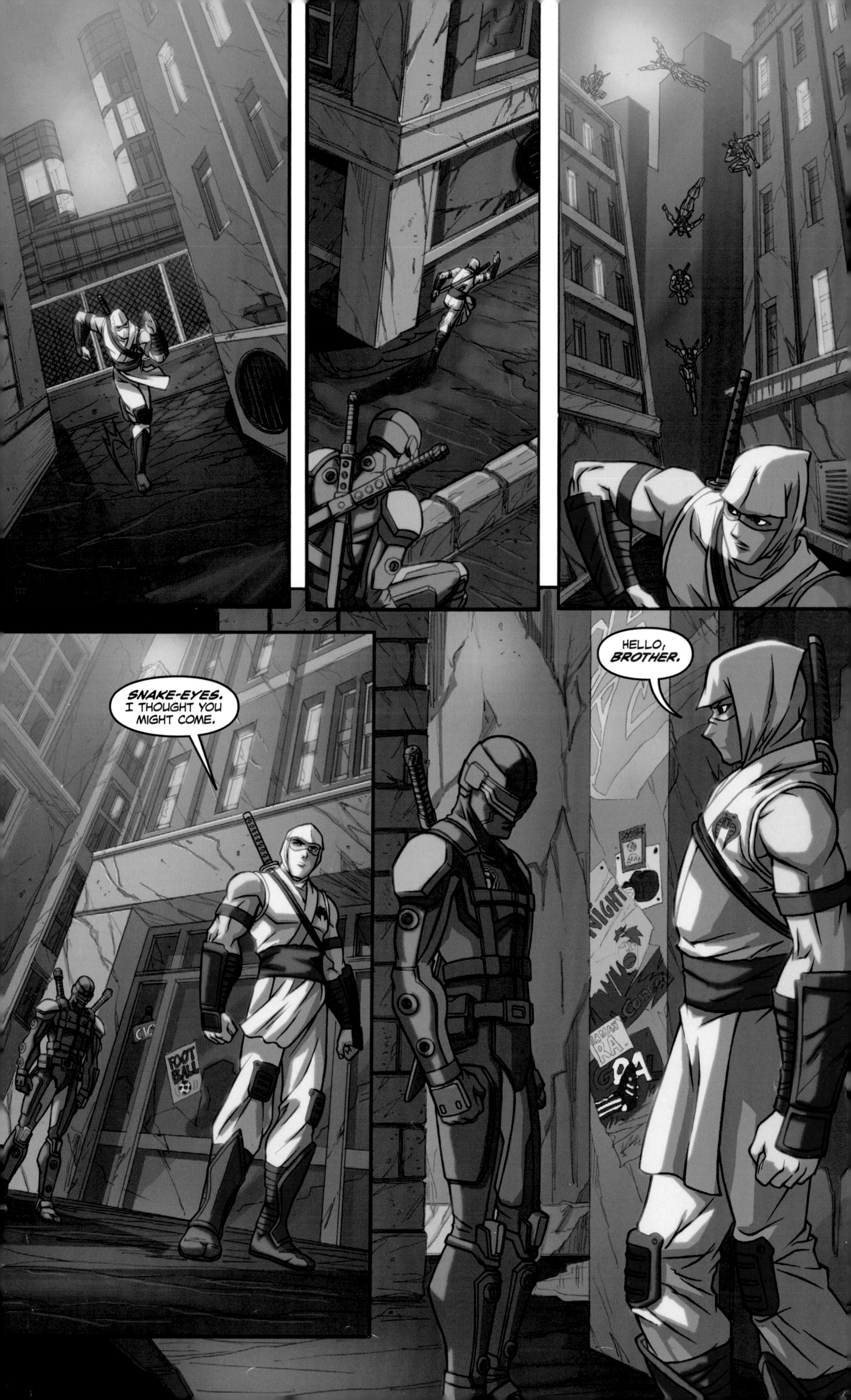

SNAKE-EYES. I THOUGHT YOU MIGHT COME.
HELLO, ***BROTHER.***

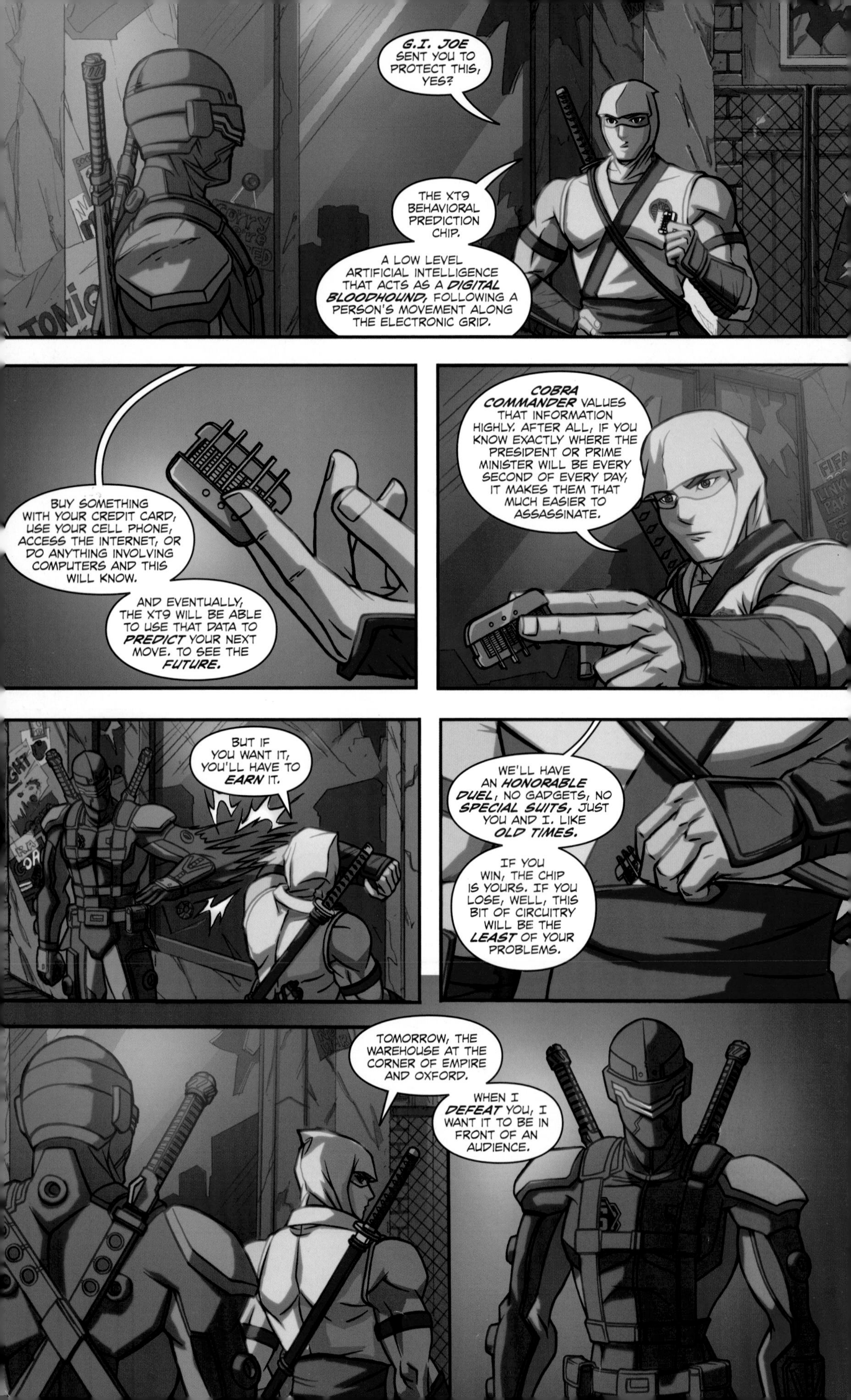

G.I. JOE SENT YOU TO PROTECT THIS, YES?
THE XT9 BEHAVIORAL PREDICTION CHIP.
A LOW LEVEL ARTIFICIAL INTELLIGENCE THAT ACTS AS A DIGITAL BLOODHOUND, FOLLOWING A PERSON'S MOVEMENT ALONG THE ELECTRONIC GRID.
BUY SOMETHING WITH YOUR CREDIT CARD, USE YOUR CELL PHONE, ACCESS THE INTERNET, OR DO ANYTHING INVOLVING COMPUTERS AND THIS WILL KNOW.
AND EVENTUALLY, THE XT9 WILL BE ABLE TO USE THAT DATA TO PREDICT YOUR NEXT MOVE. TO SEE THE FUTURE.
COBRA COMMANDER VALUES THAT INFORMATION HIGHLY. AFTER ALL, IF YOU KNOW EXACTLY WHERE THE PRESIDENT OR PRIME MINISTER WILL BE EVERY SECOND OF EVERY DAY, IT MAKES THEM THAT MUCH EASIER TO ASSASSINATE.
BUT IF YOU WANT IT, YOU'LL HAVE TO EARN IT.
WE'LL HAVE AN HONORABLE DUEL, NO GADGETS, NO SPECIAL SUITS, JUST YOU AND I. LIKE OLD TIMES.
IF YOU WIN, THE CHIP IS YOURS. IF YOU LOSE, WELL, THIS BIT OF CIRCUITRY WILL BE THE LEAST OF YOUR PROBLEMS.
TOMORROW, THE WAREHOUSE AT THE CORNER OF EMPIRE AND OXFORD.
WHEN I DEFEAT YOU, I WANT IT TO BE IN FRONT OF AN AUDIENCE.

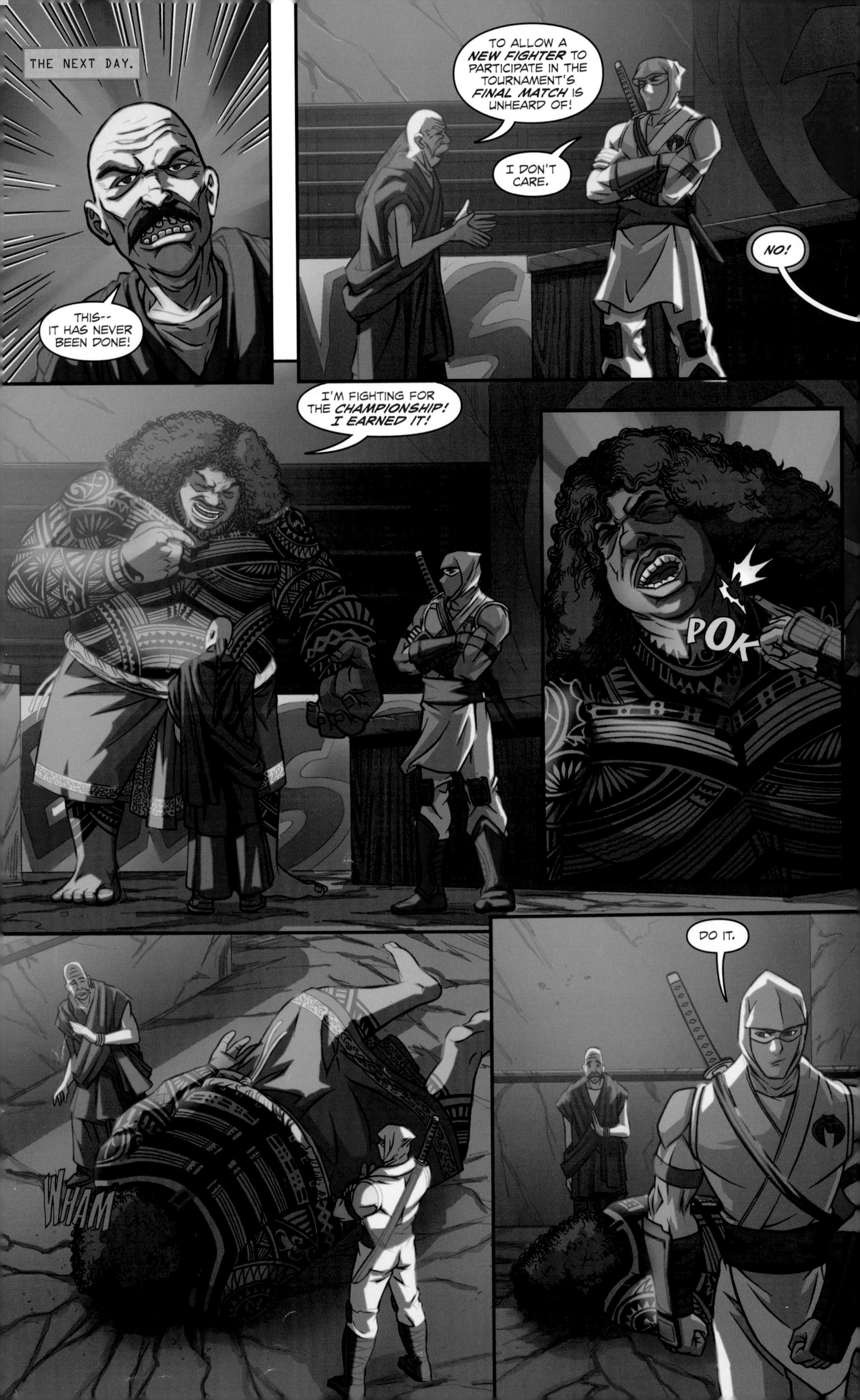
THE NEXT DAY.
THIS-- IT HAS NEVER BEEN DONE!
TO ALLOW A NEW FIGHTER TO PARTICIPATE IN THE TOURNAMENT'S FINAL MATCH IS UNHEARD OF!
I DON'T CARE.
NO!
I'M FIGHTING FOR THE CHAMPIONSHIP! I EARNED IT!
POK
WHAM
DO IT.

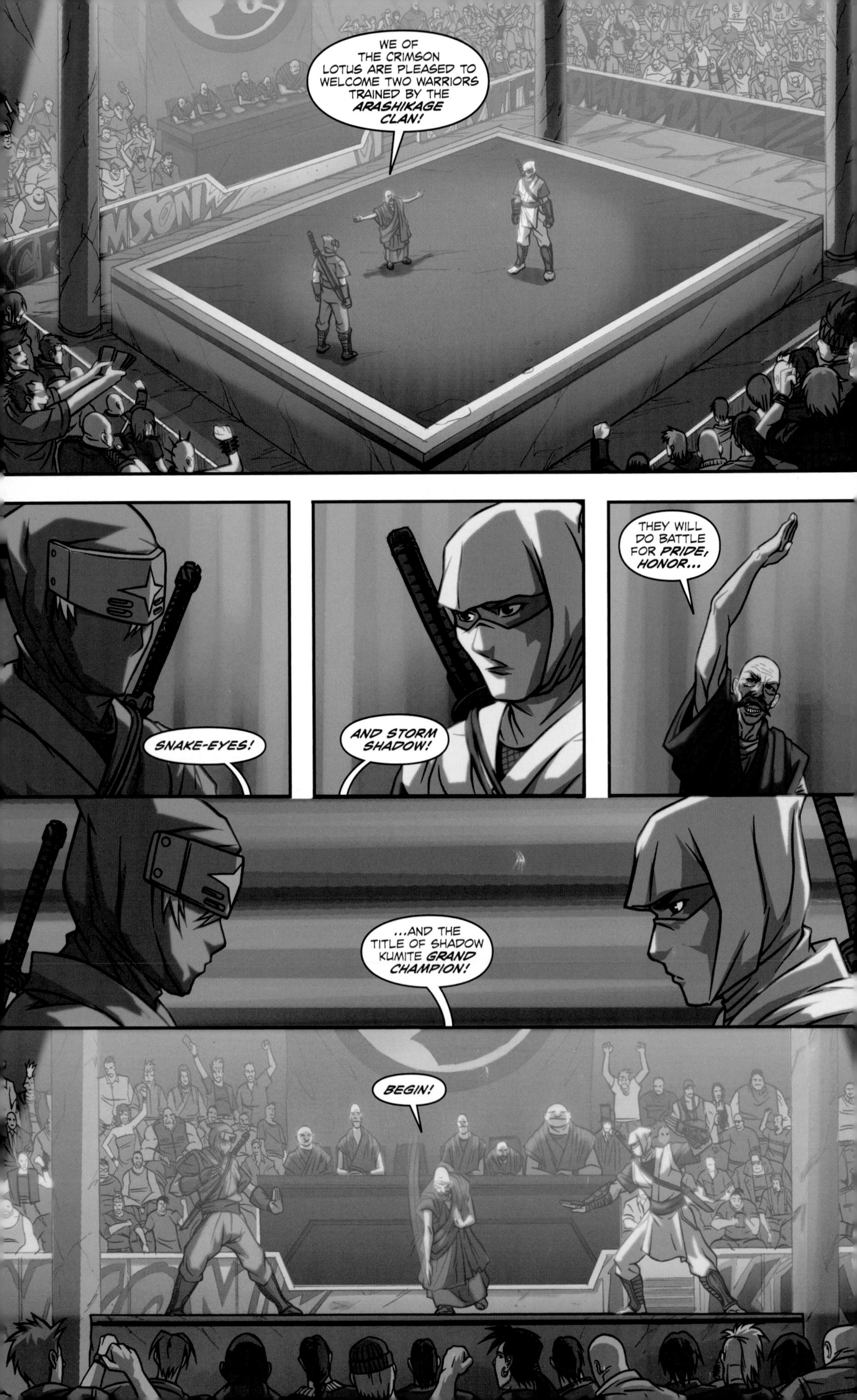
WE OF THE CRIMSON LOTUS ARE PLEASED TO WELCOME TWO WARRIORS TRAINED BY THE ARASHIKAGE CLAN!
SNAKE-EYES!
AND STORM SHADOW!
THEY WILL DO BATTLE FOR PRIDE, HONOR...
...AND THE TITLE OF SHADOW KUMITE GRAND CHAMPION!
BEGIN!

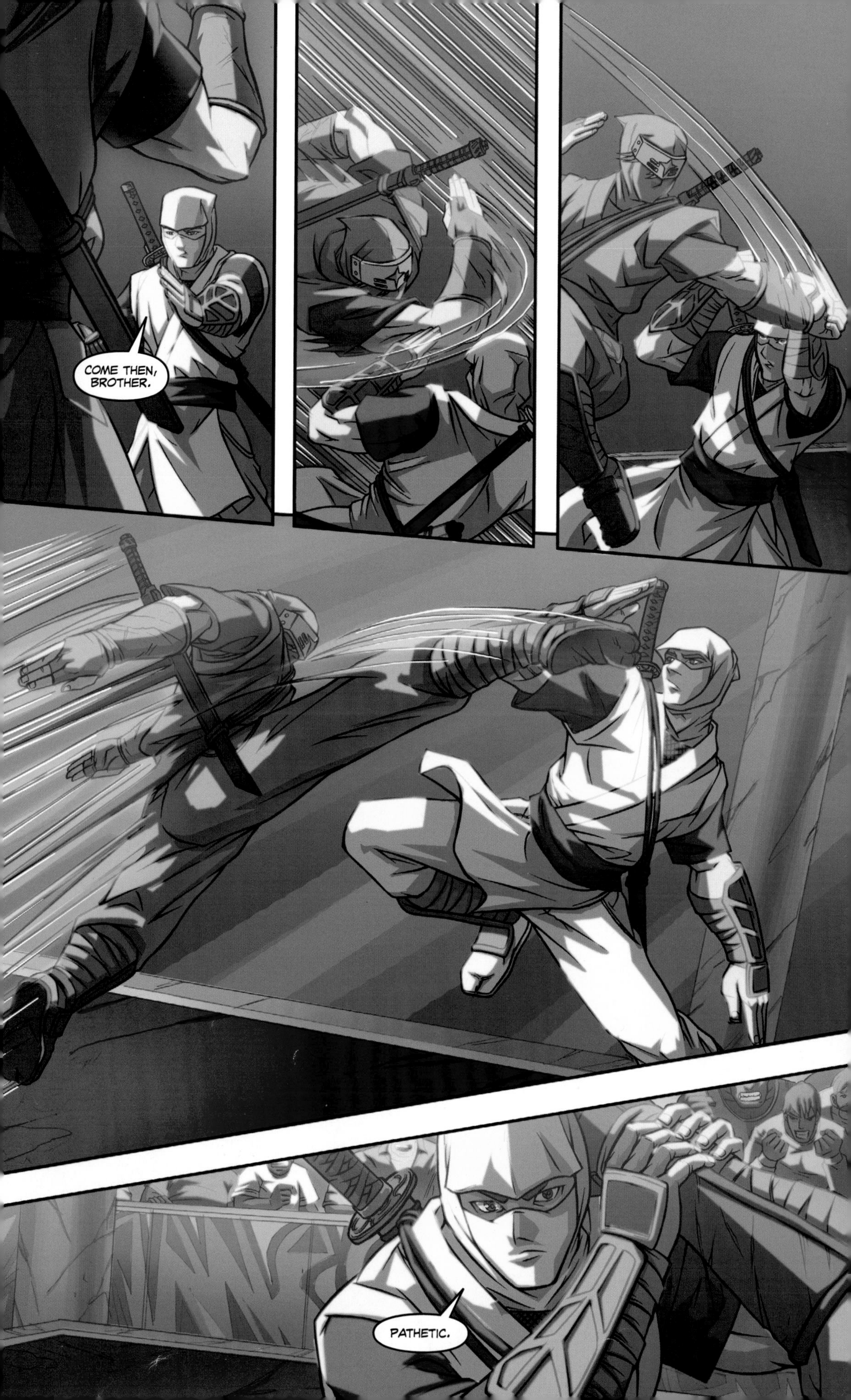
COME THEN, BROTHER.
PATHETIC.

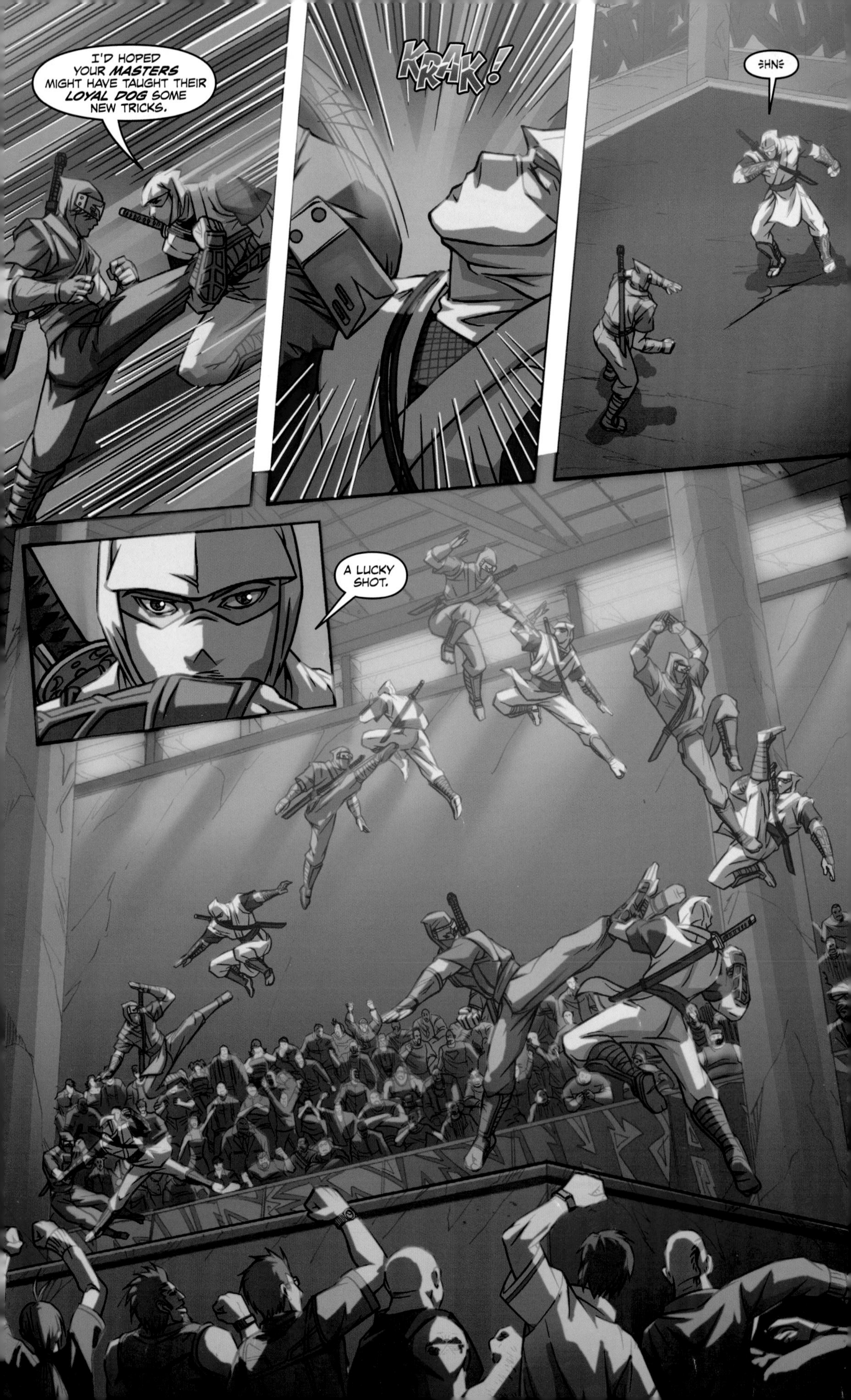
I'D HOPED YOUR MASTERS MIGHT HAVE TAUGHT THEIR LOYAL DOG SOME NEW TRICKS.
KRAK!
HHN
A LUCKY SHOT.

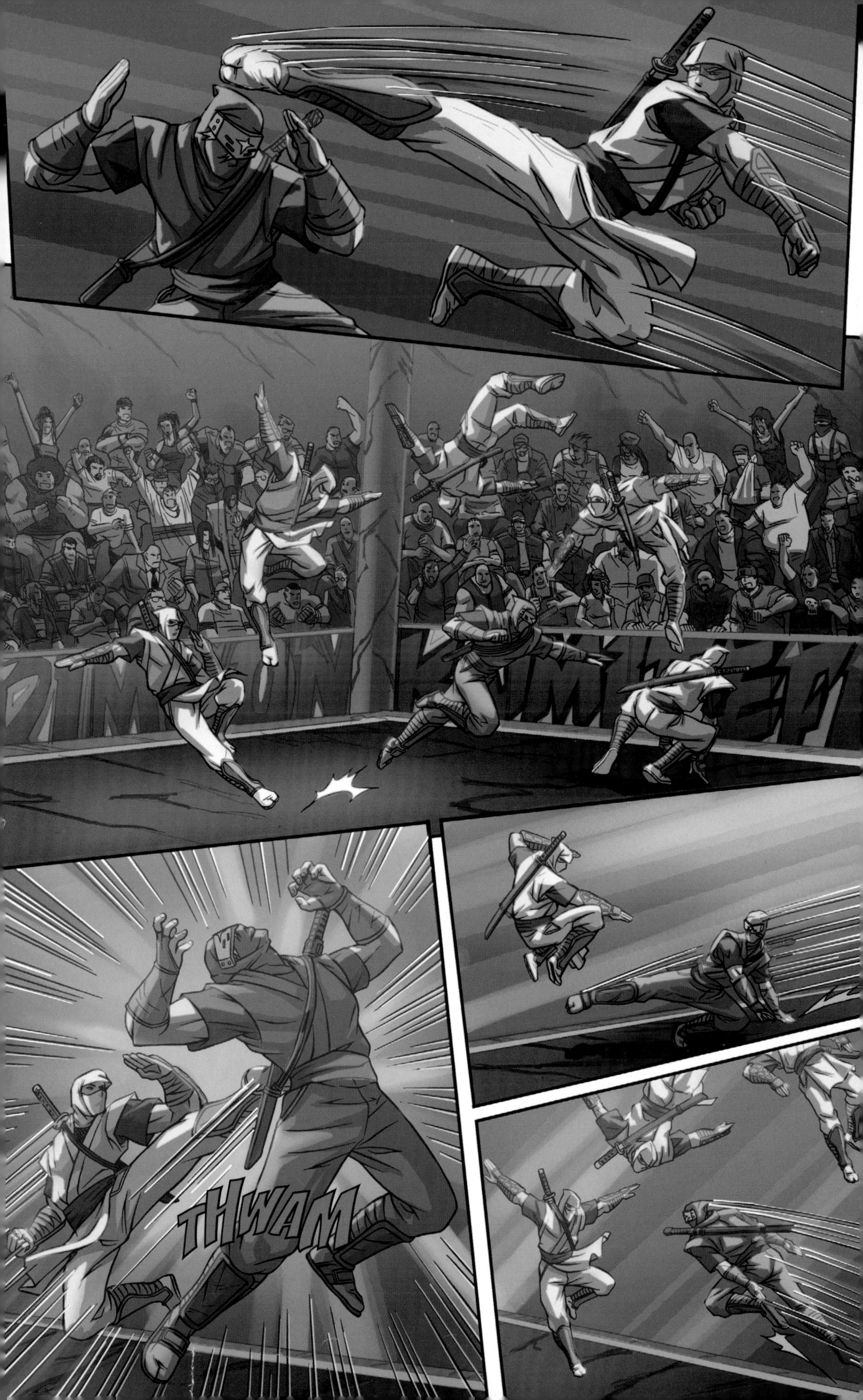
THWAM

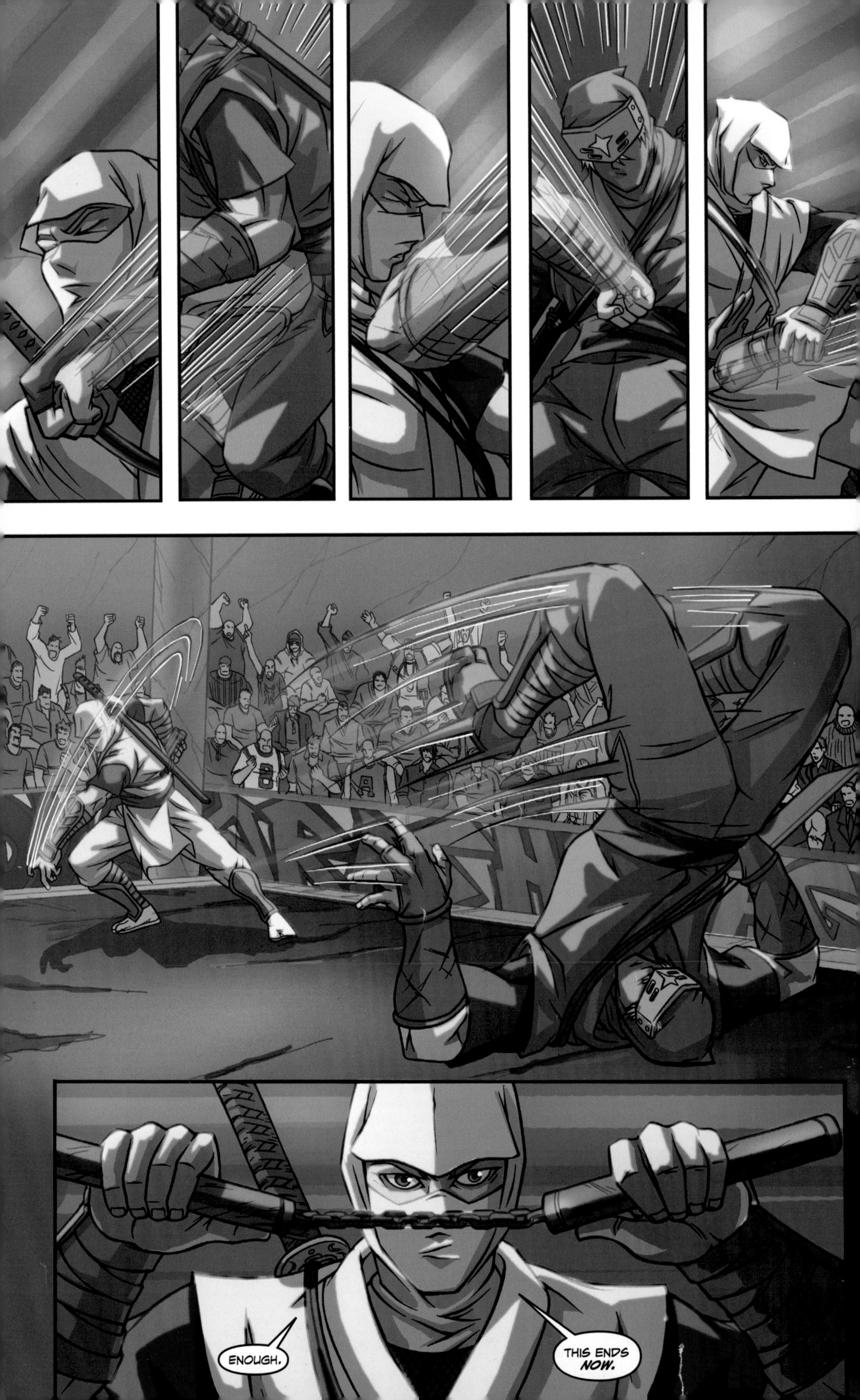
ENOUGH.
THIS ENDS NOW.

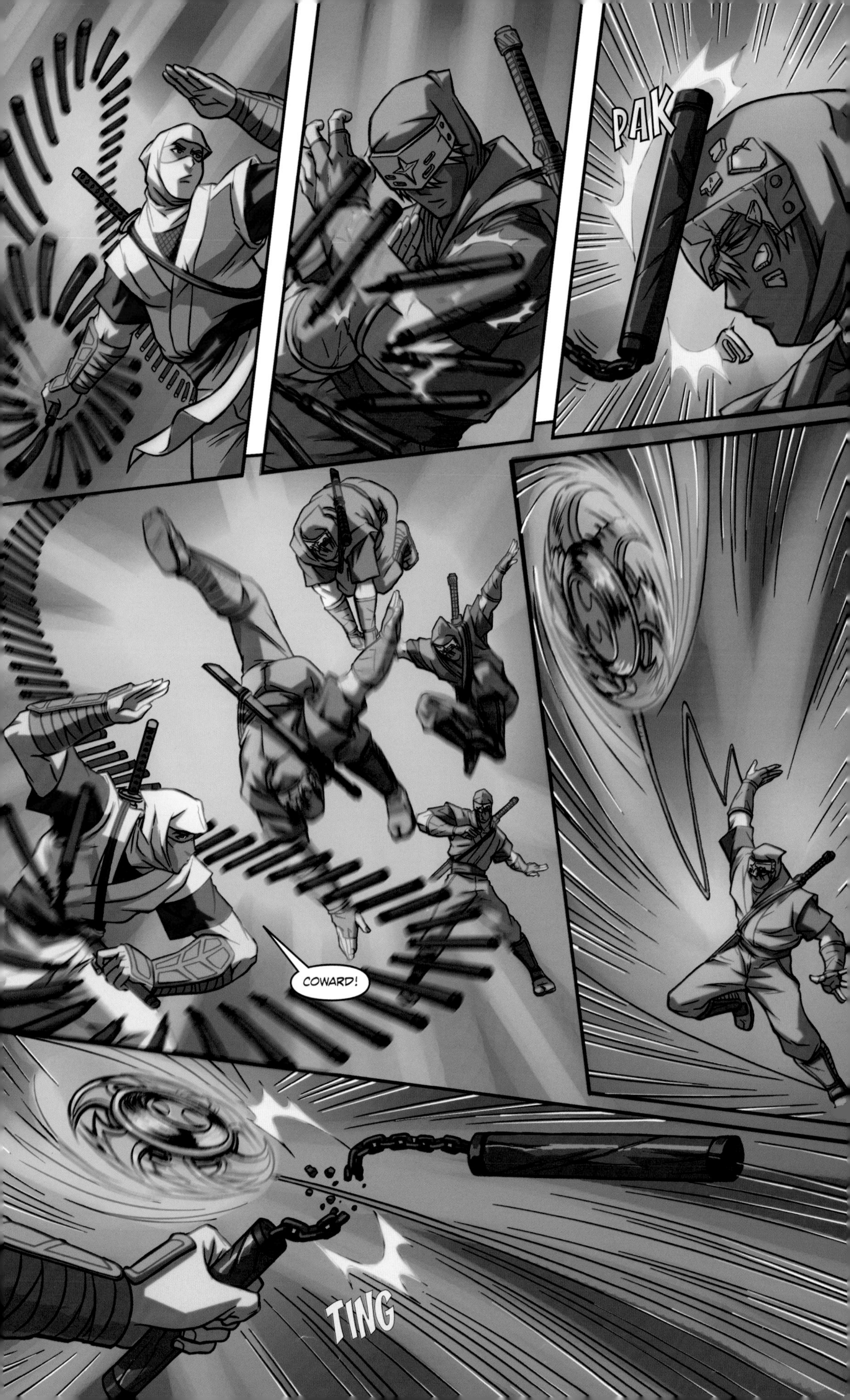
PAK
COWARD!
TING

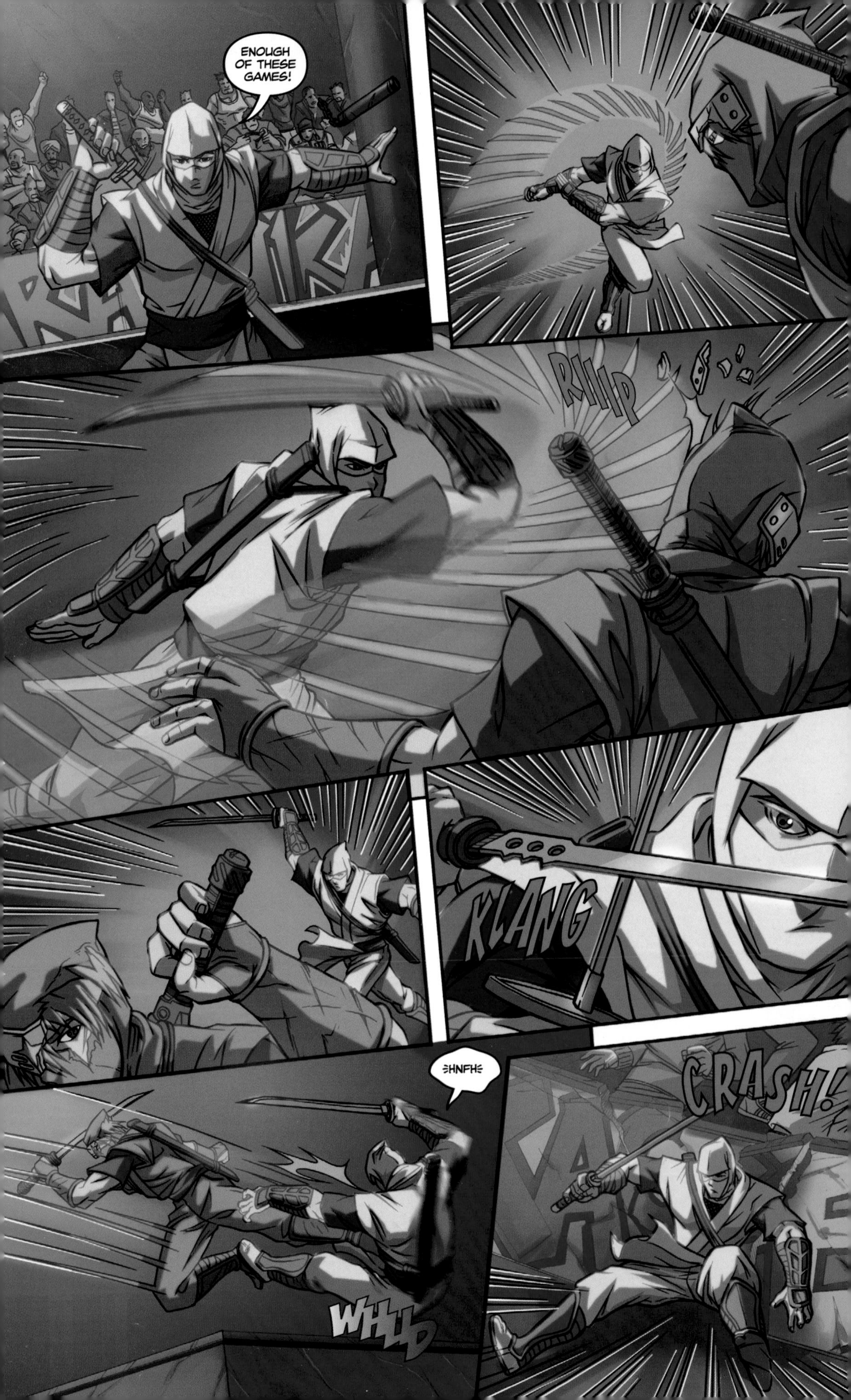

ENOUGH OF THESE GAMES!
RIIIP
KLANG
HNFH
CRASH!
WHUD

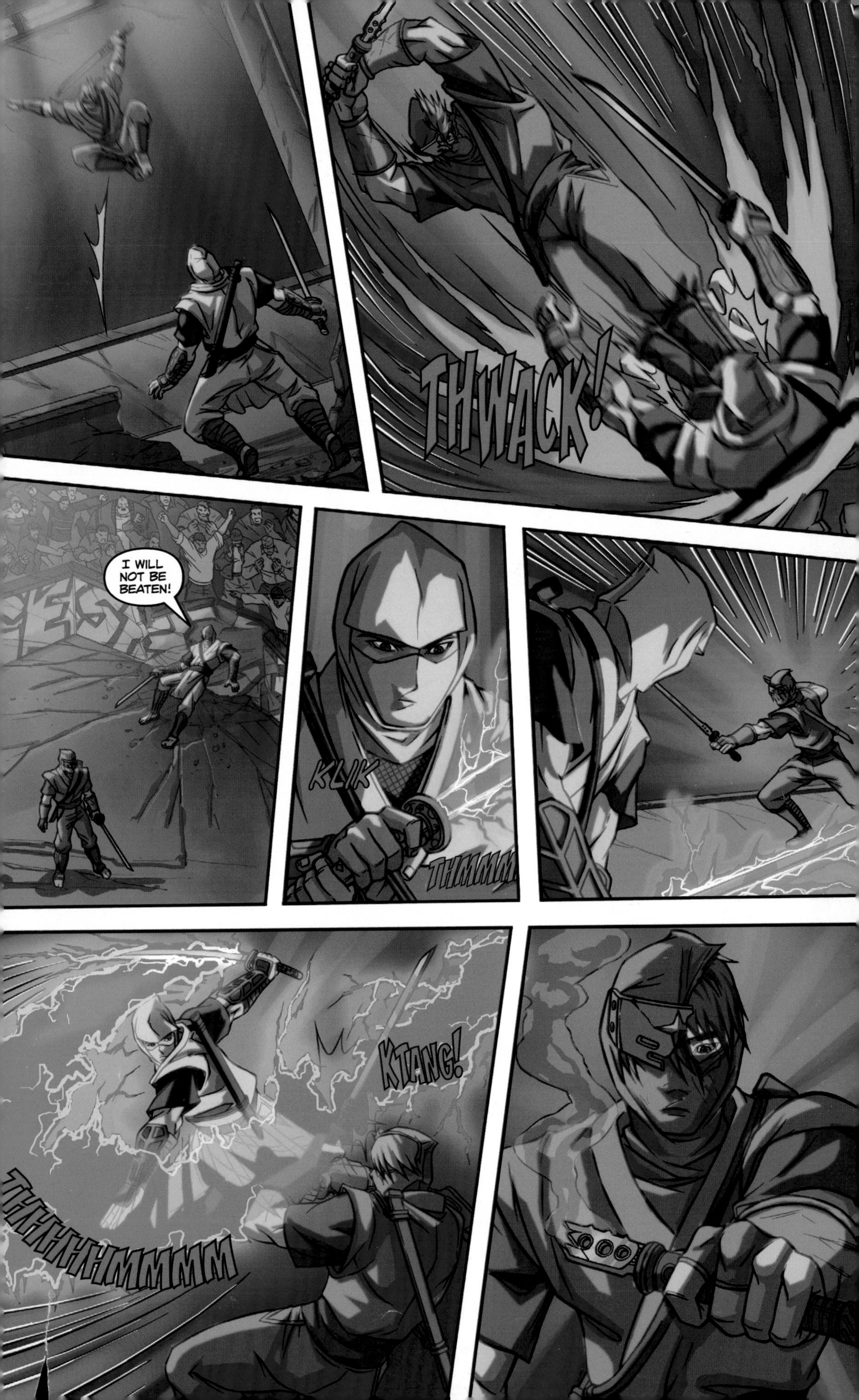
THWACK!
I WILL NOT BE BEATEN!
KLIK
THMMM
KTANG!
THHHHHMMMMM

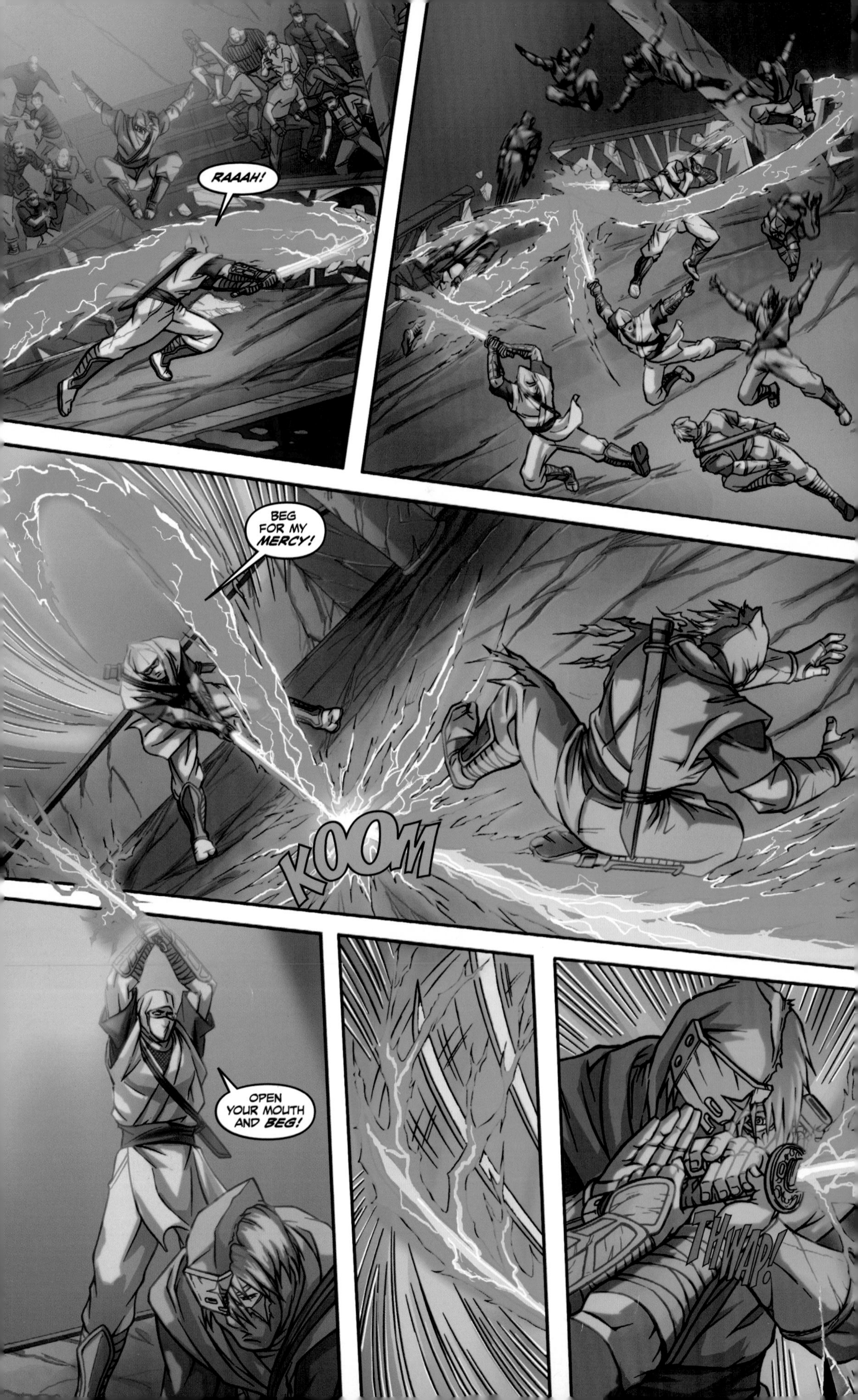
RAAAH!
BEG FOR MY MERCY!
KOOM
OPEN YOUR MOUTH AND BEG!
THWAP!

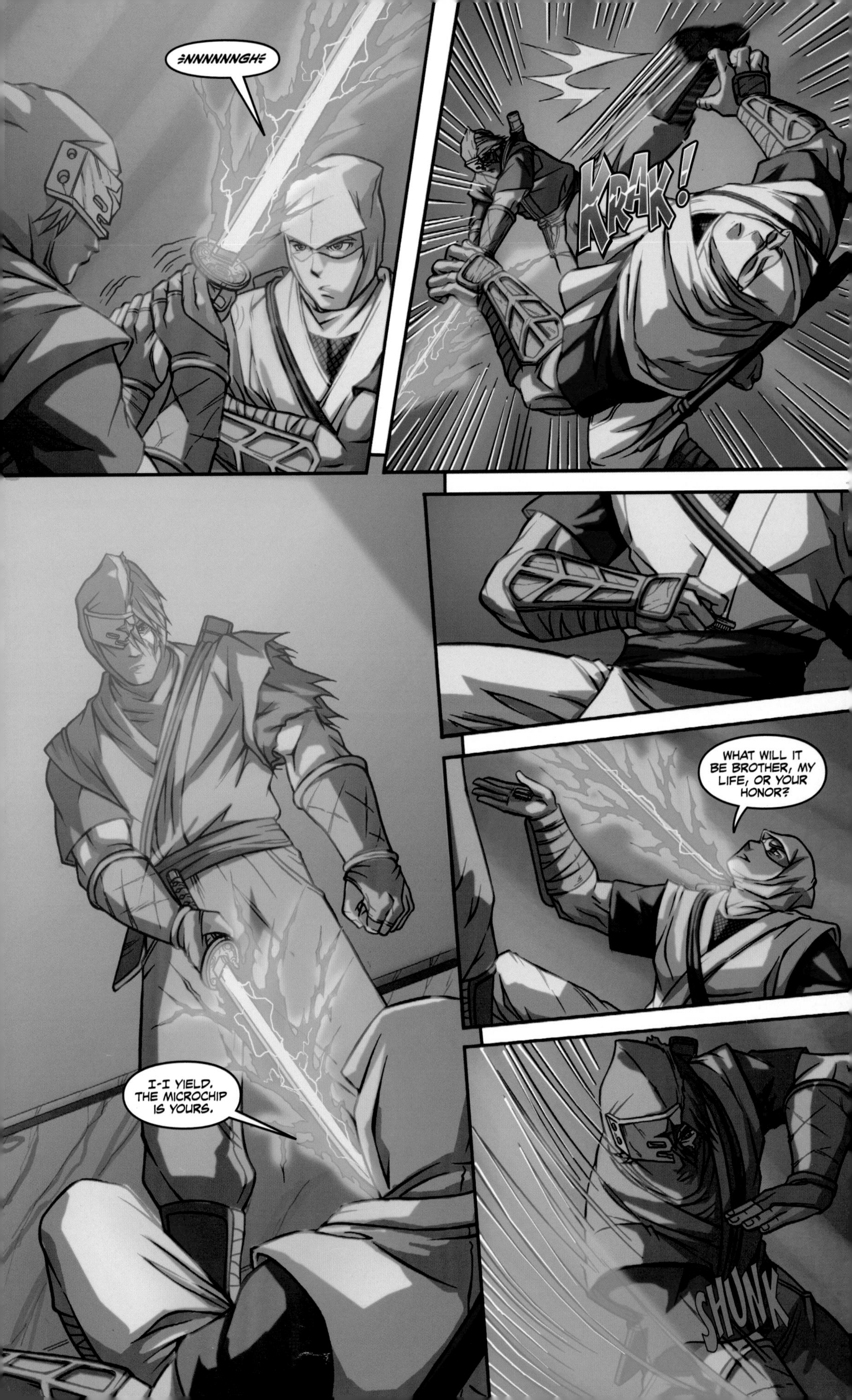
NNNNNNGH
KRAK!
WHAT WILL IT BE BROTHER, MY LIFE, OR YOUR HONOR?
I-I YIELD. THE MICROCHIP IS YOURS.
SHUNK

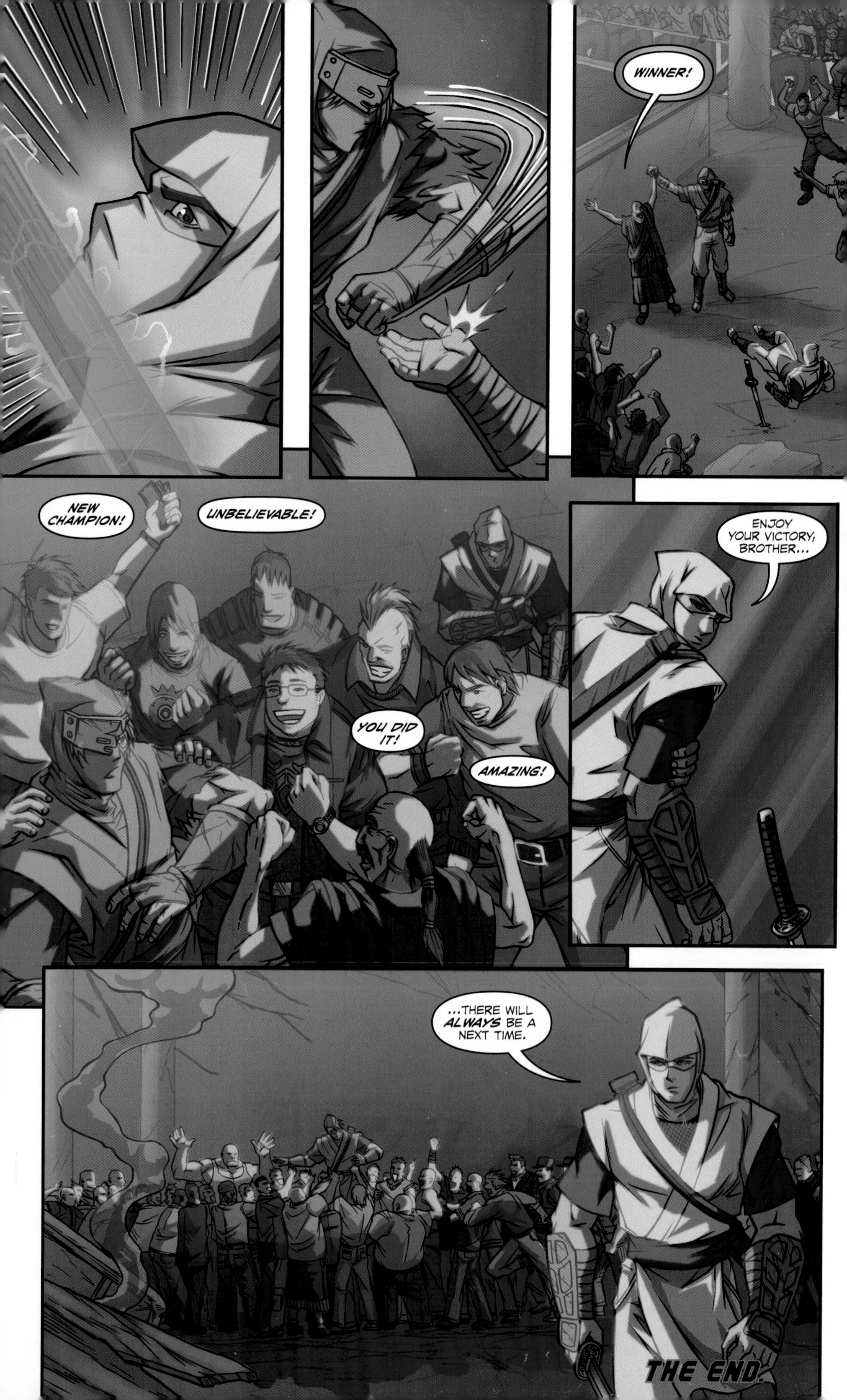
WINNER!
NEW CHAMPION!
UNBELIEVABLE!
ENJOY YOUR VICTORY, BROTHER...
YOU DID IT!
AMAZING!
...THERE WILL ALWAYS BE A NEXT TIME.
THE END.